First Novels

W9-BHF-808

Morgan and the Dune Racer

Ted Staunton
Illustrated by Bill Slavin

Formac Publishing Company Limited
Halifax, Nova Scotia

Text copyright © 2011 by Ted Staunton
Illustrations copyright © 2011 by Bill Slavin
First published in the United States in 2012

All rights reserved. No part of this book may be reproduced or transmitted in
any form or by any means, electronic or mechanical, including photocopying,
or by any information storage or retrieval system, without permission in writing
from the publisher.

Formac Publishing Company Limited recognizes the support of the Province
of Nova Scotia through the Department of Tourism, Culture and Heritage.
We acknowledge the financial support of the Government of Canada through
the Canada Book Fund for our publishing activities. Formac Publishing
acknowledges the support of the Canada Council for the Arts which last year
invested $20.1 million in writing and publishing throughout Canada.

NOVA SCOTIA
Tourism, Culture and Heritage

The Canada Council | Le Conseil des Arts
for the Arts | du Canada

Canada

Library and Archives Canada Cataloguing in Publication

Staunton, Ted, 1956–
    Morgan and the dune racer / Ted Staunton ; illustrations by Bill Slavin.

(First novels)
Issued also in electronic format.
ISBN 978-0-88780-966-8 (bound).—ISBN 978-0-88780-965-1 (pbk.)

    I. Slavin, Bill II. Title. III. Series: First novels

PS8587.T334M674 2011   jC813'.54   C2011-903325-9

Formac Publishing Company Limited
5502 Atlantic Street
Halifax, Nova Scotia,
Canada B3H 1G4
www.formac.ca

Distributed in the United States by:
Orca Book Publishers
P.O. Box 468
Custer, WA U.S.A.
98240-0468

Printed and bound in Canada.
Manufactured by Webcom in Toronto, Ontario, Canada in July, 2011
Job # 378787

Table of Contents

1

Wild Ride

VVVVVRRROOOOOOM! The Thunderbolt Dune Racer jumps. I, Commander Crunch, blast along the desert trail on planet Zorp, ahead of the evil mutant space aliens. *ZAP! ZING!* They fire at me. I weave to dodge the death rays, then *screeeeeeeCH*, I whip around the giant purple sand monster. Dirt flies; BUMPA

BUMPA BUMPA go the back wheels. Oh-oh, trouble: the rear end is sliding. It's a skid! I yank the steering. **THUNK**, the front wheel hits a boulder and — aaah, I'm in a side flip. Luckily I bounce right over in a perfect sideways 360. Gravity is lighter here on Zorp. I laugh. The sand monster doesn't even try to catch me. No one can.

Wwweeeeeeeow! That's me going by. But, *ZOW! ZOW! ZOW!* The bad guys are firing again. Luckily, all I need to do is zoom straight up Silver Mountain to the entry port of my Invincible Orbiter. I floor it. But all that happens is *RRrr RRrr Rrrr*. The Thunderbolt is slowing and now it is stopping half way up the mountain and now it is beginning to slide...back...down...

"The batteries ran out," says my friend Charlie from my play fort. He's at the top of the slide. "I told you, Morgan. They do that all the time."

"Let's get some more." I want to get back to my adventure. Do batteries go in the remote controller? Or do they go in the toy car? I pick it up. My Commander Crunch action figure falls out. The Thunderbolt is silver and blue with yellow lightning flashes.

"Naw," says Charlie. "I'm tired of that thing. Let's play football."

That's easy for Charlie to say. It's his car. He can play with it whenever he wants. He climbs down to get his football.

"Aww," I say. Then I remember my birthday is coming soon. "I am so asking for one of these for my birthday. It is so cool."

"It's dumb," growls the purple sand monster. The purple sand monster is Aldeen Hummel, in her purple sweat suit. Aldeen is over because her mom and granny are working. I don't like it when Aldeen comes over; she is not called the Godzilla of Grade Three for nothing. Plus she always disagrees with you. "Cars are dumb," Aldeen says. "Except for taxis." Aldeen's granny drives a taxi. She pushes her glasses up. She has been making faces out of sand and now some of it sticks to her nose. "Football is cool. You get to hit people." Aldeen goes to the ladder of the slide.

"You should come to my family yard sale tomorrow," Charlie says to Aldeen.

He's tossing his football in the air. "My brother is selling a helmet and shoulder pads."

I don't care about that, but I have a fantastic idea. "Well, if you're tired of your car," I say to him, "sell *it* at your yard sale." And I'll buy it, I think.

"Maybe," Charlie shrugs. I am going to Charlie's yard sale. For sure.

"Gangway," Aldeen calls. She starts down the slide. The faces she made are at the bottom. There's one with a sideways hat that looks like Charlie. There's one with witchy hair and glasses that looks like Aldeen. And there's a funny chubby one with sticking-out ears. I don't know who that is, but Aldeen is aiming right for it. **WHUMP!** She lands with her feet on either side. "I get first tackle," she says.

2

Early Bird

Saturday morning Dad takes me to Charlie's for the yard sale. He says we have to stop for coffee on the way because it is so early.

"It's not early," I say.

"Morgan, it's five after eight," Dad says. "It's early." He hasn't been up since five-thirty, like me.

So it is my dad's fault when we get to Charlie's too late. I don't know that at first. There are already cars parked and people are looking at all the stuff for sale on the driveway, but nobody is at the table where Charlie is standing.

We park and I run ahead.

"Be careful," Dad calls. My money bounces and jingles in my pocket. I stop to look both ways before I cross the road and that's when I see it. Someone tall and skinny is standing by one of the cars. The tall, skinny someone is wearing a football helmet and shoulder pads and a purple sweatsuit. Witchy hair pokes out of the helmet. The someone is carrying something the way you carry a football. Only it isn't a football. It's blue and silver

with a yellow lightning flash. It's Aldeen — and the Thunderbolt Dune Racer.

Before I can even yell, Aldeen gets into the car. It drives past me. Aldeen's granny waves. Aldeen stares. I run for Charlie's.

3

Car-napped

"You sold the car to Aldeen!" I yell at Charlie. "You knew I wanted it!"

Charlie scrunches up his face. "You said you were asking for one for your birthday. You didn't say you wanted to buy mine."

"But," I say, "but, but, but..."

By now my Dad has caught up. "Morgan,

take it easy. It's not Charlie's fault, and you do have a birthday coming up."

"Well, *she* knew I wanted it, too!"

"Then maybe you should talk to Aldeen," Dad says.

"Yeah," says Charlie. Then, "Do you want anything else?"

"NO I DON'T!" I yell. I am really mad. Charlie should be as mad as me, too. This isn't fair, so I am mad at Charlie. "Let's go see Aldeen."

"After breakfast," says Dad.

I'm not even hungry for breakfast so I don't have anything except bacon and scrambled eggs and toast and juice. Then I bike to Aldeen's.

And there she is behind the prickle bushes zooming the Dune Racer around.

My Dune Racer. She must have gotten new batteries. Aldeen is still wearing the shoulder pads and helmet, but I can see her tongue is sticking out between her teeth as she works the remote. The Racer is bouncing all over the place. Aldeen is not a good driver. Even worse, Aldeen's cat, Muscles, is chasing the Racer around, swatting at it. Or is the Racer chasing Muscles? It's hard to tell.

"Hey," I call.

Rrrrrrr goes the Racer. Aldeen grunts. She is busy steering.

"You bought my — the — car."

"So?" She still doesn't look up. Muscles yowls and spins in a circle.

"I thought you didn't even like cars."

"I don't."

"Then why did you buy it?"

"Because," says Aldeen.

"Because why?"

"Just because."

"Well, if you don't like it, why are you playing with it?"

"I'm not."

"But —"

"I'm just making sure it works. Charlie might have ripped me off."

"I'll buy it off you." I wheel my bike closer.

Aldeen steers the Dune Racer up a board onto her front porch. Muscles runs after it. Aldeen opens the door and, **Rrrrr**, drives the car inside. She pushes Muscles out of the way with her foot and goes in too. "No way," she says, and slams the door.

Muscles glares at me. I glare back. I know Aldeen has done this just to bug me. Now I am not just mad at Charlie; I am mad at Aldeen, too.

4

Secret Mission

It's midnight; my Crunch copter swoops low, zeroing in. As the chopper hovers, I climb down the rope ladder onto the castle roof. In seconds my lines are secure. I rappel down the stone wall to the window. Night vision goggles on. Look in. There it is, in a glass display case in the middle of the room.

Nothing stirs. Still, I know the room is rigged with alarms and laser-beam trip wires — except in one place. I slip suction cups on my elbows and knees. Then I freeze. A guard patrols the garden below. In my camo gear I'm almost invisible. He moves on.

It's time. I swing in the window, then **thwip-pop**, **thwip-pop**, I climb the wall and start across the ceiling.

When I'm right over the display case I release my elbows and hang from my knees. A fierce jungle cat is asleep on the floor. I'll have to be extra careful.

Rmmm. I lower the diamond glass cutter. It's tricky doing this upside down; good thing I'm a superhero. **Bzzzzzz**. The jungle cat stirs. I gulp, but keep on cutting. Crunch never quits and there's no time to lose: a guard will come by soon and I have to be out before the chopper returns. A drop of sweat plinks on the display case, then another. Finally, **Rmmm**, up comes the circle of glass. I stick it to the ceiling with bubble gum. Then, time for the spider claw. I work the controls. The claw glides down and closes gently over the priceless Thunderbolt Dune Racer. I must rescue it from the clutches of the evil witch who lives here. Slowly I raise the claw. Below me, the cat stretches. I hold my breath. It sleeps. I breathe again and here comes the car, wobbling in the claw, closer and closer and —

"AAH!" Something jabs me in the

back. Kids look up from their desks. I whip around. Aldeen still has the pointy end of her pencil pointed at me.

"What'd you get for number three?" she asks.

I look at my math work sheet. I'm not even there yet. I've been too busy with my rescue mission. I feel my face get hot. I'm not going to tell Aldeen that. I'm also not going to give her the answer, because I'm mad at her. I think I'll just say, *Wouldn't you like to know,* but then I think of two other things. One is that Aldeen gives killer noogies behind your back. The other is that, if I want my car, maybe I should try something different.

5

A New Plan

"Just a sec," I whisper over my shoulder. I do number three as fast as I can. I turn around. "Seven."

Aldeen pushes up her glasses. "That's not what I got. I got four."

She's probably right. Aldeen is better at math than me. *So what are you asking me for,* I want to say, but I don't. This is the new me; the new me with a plan. I pretend to look at my work sheet. "Oh *yeah*. You're right: four. Thanks." I swallow. Then I say, "Want to play at recess?" No one asks Aldeen to play at recess.

She nods as if it's no big deal. "Wall ball. I go first."

I hate wall ball. Never mind. "Cool," I say. "I've got two cookies, too. I'll give you one."

"What kind?"

"Chocolate chip."

"Maybe," she says, as if everyone gives her bags of cookies all the time. I take a deep breath and say, as if I just thought of it, "Hey, know what? Maybe after school you could bring the car to —"

"Nah," Aldeen says, "Cars are stupid.

Except taxis. Anyway, I don't have to go to your house this week. My mom is on nights."

"But —" I say.

"Morgan." Uh-oh. It's our teacher, Mrs. Ross. "Let's do our own work, please."

I turn back around. I am doing my own work, I think, only it's not working.

At recess we play wall ball. Aldeen wears her football helmet and wins every game, partly because she's faster than me and partly because she cheats at the score. When I say the score is wrong, she says, "Is not. I'm better than you at math." Then she kicks Simon's soccer ball all the way to the sand pit.

"Hey!" Simon says.

Aldeen doesn't even look at him. Instead, she says to me, "Where's my cookie?"

Oh, yeah. I hand it over. She eats it even faster than I eat mine. With her mouth full of cookie, Aldeen says, "Whembs yur burfdy?"

Huh? "Saturday," I say.

"I'b bebber…" she swallows, "…be invited." Her eyes go squinchy. I look to see if her noogie knuckle is sticking out. It is.

"You are," I say, fast, "for sure. I'm giving invitations tomorrow."

"Good." The noogie knuckle pops back in. Whew. Aldeen picks up the ball. "My throw. I'm winning eight – nothing."

What? I'm about to yell "No fair!"

when I remember the Racer. My Racer. I am going to be nice to Aldeen until I get that car, even if it kills me. "Ready," I say.

6

Crunched

Hand over hand, muscles bulging, Commander Crunch power-climbs the cliff to the top of the brown mountain. From there he will be able to see across the valley to the glowing light of the Zorpian Reactron screen, which answers all questions. Even now an alien Zorp giant is feeding in key data. The screen flickers.

"Okay, Morg," Dad says from the computer desk in the den. "Here we go: Thunderbolt Dune Racers."

I stand Commander Crunch up on the sofa back and go to look. Sure enough, on the computer screen is a purple Dune Racer. It is so cool. Dad clicks some more and reads. "Uh-oh," he says. "Hate to tell you, kiddo, they stopped making these in 2008. You can't get them any more."

"But that's what I really want for my birthday," I say.

"There are lots of other remote-controlled cars," Dad says.

"They're not the same." I don't know if they are or not, but I bet they aren't. And they are not the ones I want. The car Charlie had is the one I want. It's perfect.

The colour is perfect. The lightning bolt is perfect. Commander Crunch fits in perfectly. Everything about it is perfect except I don't have it. Aldeen has car-napped it and now I can't get another.

"Who knows what the day will bring," Mom says, all cheery. I know what the day will bring: not what I want. That is not fair on your birthday. "Come on," Mom says, "it's time to do your birthday invitations."

I say, "Well, I don't want to invite Charlie and I don't want to invite Aldeen." Right now I don't care what I said earlier.

"Morgan, Charlie is your best friend and Aldeen's Gran tells me you've already invited her. I was just talking to her on the phone."

Aw, rats. I feel as if I've been Crunched.

7

End of the Line

I give out invitations at school next day. I give them to Mark, Matt, Sherry, Kaely, and Will. I have almost forgotten I am mad at Charlie when I give him an invitation. I start to say, "Hey, do you wanna —"

Really fast, Charlie says, "I haveta do stuff today." I think he is mad at me because I am mad at him, so now I think I am mad at him again.

Aldeen just says, "Is there going to be cake?" Today the helmet is off but she has her shoulder pads on. She is throwing her fuzzless tennis ball at the wall. Aldeen is a hard thrower.

"Yes," I say. I mean, isn't there always? I wonder why she wants to know. Aldeen came to my last birthday because Mom made me invite her, and she dropped my cake. It flipped over and squished, candles and all. The Godzilla of Grade Three does not get invited to a lot of birthdays. I heard that is because she once bit someone's cat.

Now all she says is, "Good. I like cake. I want extra to take home."

I remember to be nice to Aldeen. "You

can have a corner piece," I say. "But you'll be over before that, right? You could come over even if your mom isn't working."

Aldeen stops throwing. "What for? I never did that before."

"Well, to play," I say.

Aldeen tilts her head. Her spidery hair bounces. "Why?"

Uh-oh. I say, "I made up this new game and it's really fun..." Sometimes my mouth gets ahead of my brain. If I don't catch up I get in trouble. "And we have to use the car to...to..." I'm almost caught up. All I have to do now is make up a game.

Before I can, Aldeen says, "Naw, car games suck. Let's play football."

All at once I don't care what my plan is. I am not playing football with Aldeen

Hummel. I can already feel her flattening me. She will probably wear those extra-big spikes she has for soccer and run right over me. And when she isn't bashing me she'll be cheating at the score. She hasn't even thanked me for the cookie or her invitation or playing with her. She's not going to bring the car over, either, just to bug me more. "No way," I say.

"Then forget it. I'll go play football with Muscles."

"I don't care," I say. "And I'm not playing wall ball either." Then I walk away.

What am I going to do now?

8

Dodging Lava Spit

For three days I go home by myself after school. I know my birthday is coming, and my party, but it doesn't help. Everything has gone wrong. First I didn't have the Racer to play with. Now I don't have anyone to play with, and I have this icky feeling it's my fault.

On the third day I'm walking home

and I see Charlie. He's playing football with Aldeen and some other kids. At least, I think they're playing football. Anyway, Aldeen has her helmet and shoulder pads on and they're all chasing her as she runs away with a football. Or is it someone's back pack? I feel even worse. I wish I wasn't mad at everybody and that they weren't mad at me. I think about my birthday tomorrow. Charlie is supposed to stay for a sleepover. What if he doesn't want to? What if nobody comes?

At home I sneak an extra cookie out to the play fort and climb up to the top. It's quiet here. Down at the bottom of the slide, the three faces that Aldeen made look up at me. I think about driving the Dune Racer around them. The faces have gotten a little crumbly, but still... They would look really cool with better eyes.

There is a bucket with marbles in it in my fort. I grab some and slide down the slide. I put marbles in the eyes and climb back up again. Now they look almost like monster faces. I slide back down and, oops, my foot lands in the middle by accident. It leaves a mark like a giant mouth. I squish more sand around to make two more mouths and climb back up.

All at once I am looking down from the cockpit of my Invincible Orbiter at a three-headed Zorpian sand dragon. Dragons will blast you out of the sky with lava spit unless you toss them glowing balls of Pluto-gunk food. You need good aim though, so the Pluto-gunk lands in

a dragon mouth. If not, you make them angry.

I aim my first throw. Yes! But it's tough to steer and throw while eating my emergency cookie ration. I miss the next few throws. Now I have to swoop down the escape chute and gather up the Pluto-gunk as fast as I can before the monster can get to me. I stuff gunk in my pockets and scramble back up the chute. There's no time to run to the ladder.

I dive into the cockpit. Lava spits at me. I take evasive action just in time. What I really need is a co-pilot. Or if there were three of us and we had my water gun, we could take turns being pilots and sand dragons. One of us could throw, one could zoom down the chute, and one could zap with my water gun for lava spit. It would be way more fun.

Except there is no one else. It's lonely on planet Zorp. What *am* I going to do?

9

Party Time?

It's time for my party and I still don't know what to do. I mean, I know I have to say I'm sorry, but I don't know exactly *how* to do it. Thinking about just plain saying it feels scary. And when should I say it? And how? I don't want to do it in front of everyone. And if I say "Sorry" to Aldeen, will she think she can noogie me if she feels like it? Do I want to say "Sorry" to Aldeen? She bought my racer even though she knew I wanted it. What if Charlie wants to stay mad anyway? What if nobody comes?

I am thinking all this while I help put up balloons and stack up paper plates and napkins. Dad is in the back yard getting games ready. Mom has the goody bags done. I have not told her anybody is mad and that they might not be coming. I am so nervous I am not even thinking about hot dogs or cake — or presents.

And then, **bing-bong**, there's the door bell and I can hear voices outside and everyone is here at once. Mom opens the door and there's Charlie and Aldeen and Matt and Mark and Sherry and Will and everyone else. Phew.

Dad comes in and hustles us all out back for games before I can say anything to Charlie or Aldeen. Outside, Aldeen cheats at the games and always butts to the front. Then, before you know it we're back inside and I'm going to open presents.

Sherry gives me a board game with flying pigs. Mark and Matt both give me cards with money. Kaely gives me two books I like. Will gives me a movie. Cool, I can watch it with Charlie tonight — if Charlie is staying. I look over. Charlie is goofing around with Matt, who has ribbon from a present around his ears.

I open Charlie's present next. It's a Commander Crunch T-shirt. I put it on right then. The last present is Aldeen's.

It's wrapped in colour comics from the newspaper. I open it carefully to save the comics to read later. Underneath is a brown box. I open it, too. Inside is the Thunderbolt Dune Racer. It looks just like it always did, except for a couple of scratches at the front that might be claw marks. *What*? I look at Aldeen.

She says, "I told you, cars are dumb. I only bought it for your birthday present."

"Hot dogs!" calls Mom.

10

Flying Pigs and
Sand Monsters

I thank everybody and we go to the back yard to eat. I have to sit beside Aldeen; I think the others are scared to. I'm thinking, *Aldeen bought the racer for me. Before she even got invited. Just as if she liked me.* Now it's not just scary, or even weird;

now I feel bad, too. I feel so bad I can't even eat my hot dog till I say it. I take a deep breath. "Thanks again for the car. Sorry I got mad."

"S'okay." She shrugs. Then she looks around and her eyes go squinchy. "I don't see any cake yet."

"Aldeen," I say, "I haven't even had my hot dog yet."

"Well, I have. Hurry up. Go see what's taking so long. I better still get a corner piece and extra. We should play football after lunch."

I am still chewing when I walk back into the house. Mom is talking on the phone. My cake is on the counter. I count the candles to make sure they are right. Then, from the den, I hear *Rrrr Rrrr,*

Rrrrrrrr. I know that sound. I look in and there is Charlie. He's playing with the Thunderbolt Dune Racer. Somehow he has it driving along, balanced on two wheels.

"Hey," I say.

Charlie looks up. His face gets red. The Dune Racer bumps into the couch and stops. "It *is* a cool car," Charlie says.

"Yeah," I say. "You can't even get them any more. We looked." It feels funny just talking after we were mad. I still have to say sorry.

"Oh." Charlie frowns. He looks at me. "Maybe we could play with it after lunch."

"I thought you were tired of it," I say.

"I was," Charlie says, "but now I like it

again. I wish I hadn't sold it."

And now I know what to say to Charlie — because I also know something else: I don't really care if I have a Dune Racer any more. I'd rather be on an interstellar action team tossing balls of Pluto-gunk to lava-spitting sand dragons on planet Zorp. So I say, "Know what? You can have it back. I shouldn't have got mad about it."

"Really?" Charlie says. "Thanks, Morgan."

"Are you still sleeping over?"

"Sure."

"Cool. 'Cause after I made up this great game where —"

"Hey, when's the cake? I thought you went for it."

I turn around. It's Aldeen. She has mustard on her chin.

Charlie says, "Morgan gave me back my Dune Racer."

Aldeen snorts. "He can't do that. I gave it to him for his birthday."

"I know," I say, "and it was really nice, but Charlie wants it even more than me and I feel bad." And I do. Now what if I just hurt Aldeen's feelings?

She says, "Well, he can't have it. I paid him for it."

"I'll pay you back," Charlie says.

Aldeen thinks. "When?"

"Tomorrow."

She thinks some more. "Okay." She turns to me. "Cake and football. And since you're giving away presents, I get the flying pigs game. We'll play it after football." She grabs the game and carries it into the hall.

I open my mouth. "But —"

"Hey," Dad calls, "where's the birthday boy? It's cake time."

"Finally," Aldeen says. "Come on."

I close my mouth. We follow her out. I, Commander Crunch, do not say a word. I'll tell Aldeen about the lava-spitting water gun later. You have to learn when to talk if you're dealing with a Zorpian sand monster. If you do, it usually works out all right in the end.

More novels in the First Novels series!

Lilly Traps the Bullies

Brenda Bellingham

Illustrated by Clarke MacDonald

Lilly faces a tough decision: choose between true friends or joining a gang of cool kids.

Mia, Matt and the Lazy Gator
Annie Langlois
Illustrated by Jimmy Beaulieu
Translated by Sarah Cummins

Mia and Matt can't wait to get to their uncle's summer cottage and find out what animal will be the star of their vacation. Will they be able to teach a lazy gator to dance?

Music by Morgan
Ted Staunton
Illustrated by Bill Slavin

Morgan has to get creative, and sneaky, if he wants to play music instead of floor hockey. He crafts a plan to swap places with Aldeen — but how long will they pull it off before they get caught?

Daredevil Morgan

Ted Staunton

Illustrated by Bill Slavin

Will Morgan be brave enough to try the GraviTwirl ride at the Fall Fair? Can he win the "Best Pumpkin Pie" contest, or will Aldeen Hummel, the Godzilla of Grade Three, interfere?

Raffi's For the Birds

Sylvain Meunier

Illustrated by Élisabeth Eudes-Pascal

Translated by Sarah Cummins

Raffi wants to save the birds by protesting the destruction of the trees they nest in. While he may have trouble walking, he has lots of ideas, and friends ready to help!